Please return/renew this item by the last date shown.
Item may also be renewed by the internet*

https://library.eastriding.gov.uk

* Please note a PIN will be required to access this service
- this can be obtained from your library.

For Oswin xx — G.H.

For Eunice xx — A.R.

First published 2021 by Nosy Crow Ltd

The Crow's Nest, 14 Baden Place

Crosby Row, London, SE1 1YW

www.nosycrow.com

ISBN 978 1 83994 154 2 (HB) • ISBN 978 1 83994 155 9 (PB)

Nosy Crow and associated logos are trademarks

and/or registered trademarks of Nosy Crow Ltd.

Text by Goldie Hawk

Text copyright © Nosy Crow 2021 • Illustrations copyright © Angie Rozelaar 2021

The right of Goldie Hawk to be identified as the author and of

Angie Rozelaar to be identified as the illustrator of this work has been asserted.

A CIP catalogue record for this book is available from the British Library.

Printed in China

Papers used by Nosy Crow are made from wood grown in sustainable forests.

1 3 5 7 9 8 6 4 2 (HB) • 1 3 5 7 9 8 6 4 2 (PB)

Goldie Hawk   Angie Rozelaar

We're Going on a Present Hunt

nosy crow

We're going on a present hunt.
We're going to find a good one.
What a beautiful night!
We're not scared.

Uh-oh . . .

Christmas trees!

Tall, spiky Christmas trees.
Can't go over them.
Can't go under them.
Can't go around them.

Got to go **through** them!

Rustle, rustle!

Rustle, rustle!

Rustle, rustle!

We're going on a present hunt.
We're going to find a good one.
What a beautiful night!
We're not scared.

Uh-oh . . .

Reindeer!

Friendly, hungry reindeer.
Can't go over them.
Can't go under them.
Can't go around them.

Got to go **through** them!

Gobble-munch!

Gobble-munch!

Gobble-munch!

We're going on a present hunt.
We're going to find a good one.
What a beautiful night!
We're not scared.

Uh-oh . . .

Carol-singers!

Joyful, noisy carol-singers.
Can't go over them.
Can't go under them.
Can't go around them.

Got to go **through** them!

Fa-la-la!

Fa-la-la!

Fa-la-la!

We're going on a present hunt.
We're going to find a good one.
What a beautiful night!
We're not scared.

Oh, wow . . .

A toyshop!

A bright, busy toyshop.
Can't go over it.
Can't go under it.
Can't go around it.

BOO

Got to go **through** it!

Jingle-jangle!

Jingle-jangle!

Jingle-jangle!

But wait . . . what's that?

A BEAR!

Quick, let's go!

Back through the toyshop.

Jingle-jangle!   Jingle-jangle!   Jingle-jangle!

Back through the carol singers.

Fa-la-la!   Fa-la-la!   Fa-la-la!

Back through the reindeer.　Gobble-munch!

Gobble-munch!

Gobble-munch!

Back through the Christmas trees.

Rustle, rustle!

Rustle, rustle!

Rustle, rustle!

All the way back with . . .

...a **PRESENT** for the baby.
Merry Christmas, everyone!